MW00892200

# My Wild Garden Zoo

## By Therese Hutchinson

RIVERBEND
PUBLISHING

There's an antelope in the cantaloupe...
and bears in the huckleberries.

There's a big black crow in every row...
and a mule deer we call "Larry."

In yellow squash the bluebirds slosh...
and ants are lookin' busy.

Near the beans it surely seems...
goats munch 'till they are dizzy!

A hungry moose eats kale with a goose.
I hope he stays out of the beets!
A badger last Monday, left until Sunday,
he really prefers to eat meat.

We have tomatoes and lots of potatoes
where an elk was taking his nap.

When coyote pups woke him up, we almost had a mishap!

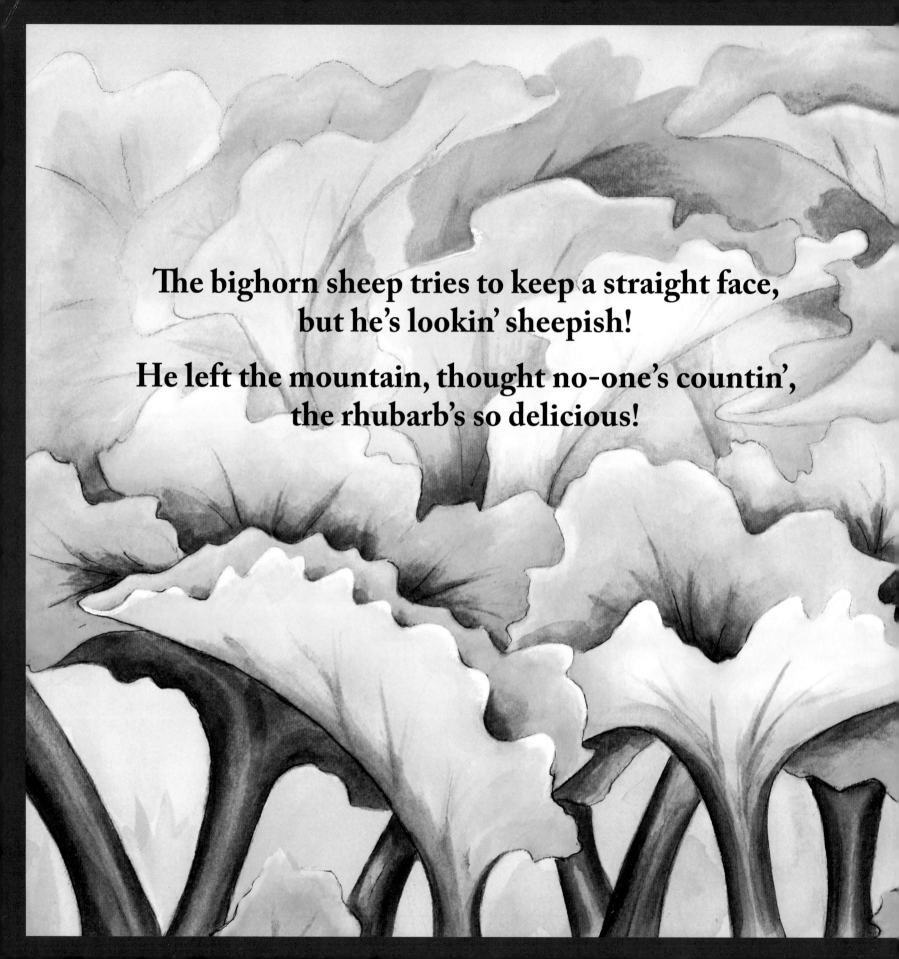

The bighorn sheep tries to keep a straight face,
but he's lookin' sheepish!

He left the mountain, thought no-one's countin',
the rhubarb's so delicious!

There's pumpkins and peas, but somebody
PLEASE tell the whitetail my hound dog saw...
he must not ravage the rows of cabbage
or Grandpa won't have his coleslaw!

The bison named Bert ate onions with dirt.
I'm really not sure he was thinkin'!

His friends all backed up, the squirrels all cracked up...
a yawn showed Bert's breath was STINKIN'!!

Cute gray bunnies think it's funny,
but I don't think Grammy can bear it!
Those silly rabbits have a bad habit
of dining on all of her carrots!

A gopher digs tunnels, except when there's sun,
he'll sit up and sing on his hill.

Then there's the beaver, I couldn't believe her!
She chomped down the pickling dill!

The raspberries are prickly, and you'll end up sticky,
but the jelly Mom makes is worth it.
So you'd better get pickin' 'cause magpies are fixin'
to munch and they'll eat every bit!

I noticed an eagle, looking quite regal,
surveying the entire scene.

He saw from his perch, up high in the birch,
the butterfly on the scarecrow's jeans.

A robin and chickadee seeing what could be,
decided to join the feast!

They ate and ate 'till they saw through the gate,
the party's about to cease!!

They spotted my Clyde who opened up wide
with a howl that rattled your bones!

The animals scattered,
but all that mattered
to Clyde was guarding
his home!

Now the loons sing a tune...
by the light of the moon.

Another day's done at our farm.

I've had a great view of my wild garden zoo from my favorite place in the barn.

## Dedication

*For my beautiful grandchildren Ellianna, Maisy, Adrienne, Chase, Ryder, Gunnar, Brynnlee and Hope. You are the joy of my life! I hope you always treasure and enjoy our wildlife as much as Grandpa and I do!*

## Acknowledgements

A special thank you to my husband Roger and our family for your encouragement and support, and many thanks to our "other" family at Main Street Market for taking on the extra responsibilities so I could disappear for a while to finish the illustrations. Also, to Joanne Simpson, a most gifted water colorist and teacher, thank you for giving me wings!

*My Wild Garden Zoo*
Copyright © 2015 by Therese Hutchinson

Art and text by Therese Hutchinson

Published by Riverbend Publishing, Helena, Montana

ISBN 13: 978-1-60639-086-3

Printed in China.

1 2 3 4 5 6 7 8 9 0 EP 22 21 20 19 18 17 16 15

All rights reserved. No part of this book may be reproduced, stored, or transmitted in any form or by any means without the prior permission of the publisher, except for brief excerpts for reviews.

Cover and page design by Sarah Cauble, www.sarahcauble.com

Riverbend Publishing
P.O. Box 5833
Helena, MT 59604
1-866-787-2363
www.riverbendpublishing.com